Table of Contents

Content Warning

This book is solely for people who are over the age of legal adulthood due to its sexual content. There are themes with a lot of bad words. All characters are well over the age of eighteen.

"My son's fingers were embedded in my pussy as I spoke to my spouse. "When are we going to come to an end?"

-- Ellen

Mom and I were exhausted as we came to terms with our post-orgasmic euphoria.

-- Joel

"Oh my god, I'm cuming on your fingers, mommy's cuming. Oh god, what have we done? "

-- Ellen

It's time to stop calling you "squirt," She remarked. I prefer the name "Alpha - Gusher."

--Tasha

The Road Trip Secret

Complete Series Box Set

(Mother and Son's Secret)

Karena Donger

Copyright © 2022 Karena Donger

This is a work of fiction. Names, characters, places, and incidents either are the product of the author's imagination or are used fictitiously, and any resemblance to actual persons, living or dead, business establishments, events, or locales is entirely coincidental.

This ebook is licensed for your personal enjoyment only. This ebook may not be re-sold or given away to other people. If you would like to share this book with another person, please purchase an additional copy for each recipient. If you're reading this book and did not purchase it, or it was not purchased for your use only, then please return to your favorite ebook retailer and purchase your own copy. Thank you for respecting the hard work of this author.

ISBN: 978-1-63750-301-0

Free Bonus

Grab My "At The Beach (Erotic Romance Story)" Ebook For FREE!

Today you can grab your copy of my Free Erotic Romance story e-book titled – **At The Beach**. Best of all, it won't cost you a thing.

Download and Subscribe for Free book, giveaways, and new releases by **Karena Donger.**

Click the image above to **Download the Book**, and also Subscribe for Free books, giveaways, and new releases by me.

Or Follow the link below;

https://mayobook.com/karenadonger

As my subscriber, you will enjoy more free books exclusive to subscribers only, plus **Free Giveaways**. Wait no further, join my growing number of book lovers, and let's connect.

Chapter 1

The Road Trip

In August, we spent the morning getting the car ready for a road trip. Joel, one of our children, was getting ready to head off to college. When I got out of bed, it was already a balmy ninety degrees outside. **Joel** and I worked up a sweat as we piled everything into the car. I couldn't fit any more in my trunk or the backseat. Finally, Joel returned to the house to retrieve all of his personal belongings.

I could hear him coming out of the house as he walked down the driveway. Turning back, I saw him lugging a 42-inch flat-screen TV with him.

"Where will you put the television?" My ears perked up when I heard his dad ask.

In the end, I'm not sure why, but I don't want to give it up. Is there anything we can do to reorganize the backseat?

I took a peek behind the wheel. *"It's not likely, son,"*

said the father. **Joel** took a peek inside the vehicle. A middle seat in the front is an option, he said.

We agreed on a time and on a place. Is your mother going to sit there, too?

I could tell he was racking his brains for an answer by the look on his face. He said, *"I've got an idea"* and then proceeded to explain it further.

He let himself out of the car through the passenger door. The television was placed at the center of the car seat by him.

Once inside, he sat down. *"There's plenty of room."* Mom, please take a seat here beside me.

To my son's dismay, I sat next to him. In order to get in, I had to sit down, but the door wouldn't shut properly. I'm no longer a fat woman. I'm a slender five-foot-ten-inch woman who weighs no more than a hundred pounds.

My son was taking up the entire space at the back seat. The young man was already well over six feet tall and weighs about 180 pounds.

Rather than me, it's you who's taking up all the space. This isn't going to succeed. *"When we come to visit you, we'll bring the television with us."*

When I got out of the car and stood by the door, he said, *"No way."*

"Joel, make a decision. It's getting hot out here." I said.

Joel smiled as he nodded and smiled back at me. You're welcome to sit on my lap, mum.

His father told him, *"Joel, it's a five-hour drive to your college."*

It's true, but my mother does not have a huge body frame, I can lap her conveniently sir.

Mom, what do you think? *"Would it be okay if you sat on my lap mum?"* **Joel** asked.

"Let me take a seat on your lap, then." I agreed.

Even if I'd like to stop at a rest stop if the situation gets too uncomfortable. I said this while staring at my spouse. *He nodded his head in agreement.*

It's time to take a shower and get ready for the road trip, right? My asked asked.

There wasn't a lot of time spent in the shower. The five-hour-long ride on my son's lap necessitated that I wear something comfy. My jean pants would be too uncomfortable.

In addition, the weather was unbearably hot. I looked in the closet. While sorting through my wardrobe, I came across a summer dress. There were no sleeves on the short side. In the front, it was buttoned up. I undid the buttons and slipped it on.

As soon as I finished buttoning it, I realized how much of my bra it revealed. I removed it once again. I removed my bra and re-adjusted my dress.

I checked my reflection in the bathroom mirror. I didn't really need a bra at all. My tits were still perky despite being at the age of *thirty-nine*.

It was a short dress. My thighs were barely touched by it, as the dress was barely covering half of my thigh. *Pear-shaped white panties* were all I needed to complete the look.

For one last time, I examined my reflection. I had a thought. *"As the mother of a twenty years son, I appeared to be in good shape. I'm confident that my husband still appreciates the way I look."* Five times a week, he fucks me real good!

The car's horn sounded. "puuuuuurrh"

As soon as I got downstairs, I shut and locked the front door of the house, and headed out the door to the car.

My son was already sitting in the car's back seat. I sat down on his lap and swung my legs into the car.

I looked down and *my thighs were barely covered by my clothing because it's short.* It climbed to a respectable altitude of my thigh. Shorts and a t-shirt were all my son had on. I slammed the door of the car.

Wearing this dress made me happy and comfortable as a beautiful sexy woman.

My son's bare legs touched the back of my legs.

"How are you doing, hope you can bear my weight?" My son was the one I turned to for an answer.

"Okay, mum, you don't weigh much. There is no problem at all."

To my husband's left as we looked over the TV. *Is there enough room for you to drive honey? I asked him,* and he said **yes**.

I could only see his head. *"Can you even see me?"* I laughed as I asked.

"Only your head, dear." "Are you comfortable? he asked."

As I sat on my son's lap, I squirmed around. It's not a problem for me at all.

My husband turned on the radio to play music. A few minutes into the music, something abrasive had begun to gnaw at me. It didn't go away even after I shifted my body position, and adjusted my ass.

In addition, I noticed that my son had been unusually silent. In the beginning, "*I couldn't figure it out.*" I had a thought.

It dawned on me that my feelings were not what they seemed to be at the time. <u>My son was having a serious erection by sitting on his lap</u>, I really didn't think about giving him an erection by sitting on his lap.

Even now, I could sense its expansion.

"*My gosh,*"

I muttered under my breath.

The question is, "*How big will it get?*" I couldn't help but wonder what was going through his mind.

Does he think I can't feel it in my ass?

My gaze was drawn to my legs. There was a slight rise in the skirt of my dress. *I was almost able to see my panties.*

On either side of me, I could see my son's hands resting on the seats.

I was curious if he had noticed how high my dress had ridden up on the back of the chair. I've come to appreciate having my dress so high. Knowing I could give my son a hard-on to make me feel good.

It was just over an hour into our journey. Even with the remaining time, only four hours remained.

In order to avoid my husband noticing how high the skirt of my dress was, I made sure he couldn't see the length of my skirt. He couldn't see anything because of the television in between.

My son's body began to *wiggle,* and I knew it was him.

My ass ended up completely covered on his dick as he did it. I was hoping he would at least give it a go.

Inquiring about how he was doing back there *"son, how are you doing there"*.

In response to the question,

"I am Okay mom", *"How are you feeling, Mom?"*

I told him, *"I like what I'm feeling."*

I answered him - *"Are your arms getting tired where you have them?"*

"Yea, it's a little uncomfortable,"

Weird, to say the least.

To see whether it felt better, I took both of his hands and placed them on my bare thighs, saying;

"Is that better"

Yeah, it's much better and more comfortable; He said.

"That's much better, Yes."

I lowered my gaze and took a closer look. When he placed his hands on my thighs, I made sure they were palms down instead of up.

I could feel his thumbs pressing into the crooks of my thighs, very close to my panties. It had a pleasing appearance to me. I wished he'd put his hands on my pussy and stroked it.

In my mind, he couldn't do it. I wanted him to feel me more and more as I felt his hands on me. In my hands, he was mine. All of that appeared to be innocent. I began scrubbing his palms. Like every other mother, I wanted to do something special. My hubby was driving and more focused on the road as the situation was getting sweeter at the back seat of the car.

Having my son's hands on my body was a pleasant thought, especially with my husband around. His hands were moving up my thighs as I stroked them. He didn't resist. His fingers were still on my thighs as he placed his hands on my skirt.

I moved up slightly so that I could raise my skirt a bit. With my skirt, he moved his hands. *My pants were clearly visible when I lowered my gaze. His fingers were just a few centimeters away from my pussy.*

In order to get him to put his right hand on my panties, I raised it, and placed his hand on my panty-covered pussy.

This is where his hand was left. My legs were a little open.

When I did, he reached out and grabbed hold of my panties. I grabbed his hand and pressed it against my panties. My son's hand was now resting on my pussy, which was dripping wet.

I could tell that I was getting wet already. I was starving for more.

When I took my hand off of him, he continued to hold on. He wasn't even fumbling with it. Just letting his hands rest on my pantie-covered pussy, that's all. I waited for him to start moving his fingers.

Nothing happened. Maybe he was afraid to. I knew how to fix that.

When I grabbed his hand, I shifted it up to the top of my underwear. It was only then that I held his hand against mine and allowed him to softly slide his fingers between my undergarments and my exposed fleshy pussy.

When his fingertips finally touched the top of my swollen, pussy lips, **I froze.**

I continued to press my fingers into his palm. The only way he could feel my genitals was if I could slide his hand all the way between my legs and beneath my underpants.

Both of our hands were squeezing out of my pants since they were too small. Then, finally, I felt him try to move his hand farther down so that he could locate my pussy entry point.

My son's hand remained on my genitals as I removed my hand from under my underpants.

With both hands, I lifted my hips and dragged my pants down to my knees. As soon as I did this, I felt

Joel move his hand so he could insert his fingers into my pussy.

Because of my underwear, I couldn't get my legs out wide enough for him to truly get a feel for me.

Joel grabbed hold of my pants with his other hand before I could even begin to remove them from around my ankles.

I swung my legs up to make it easier for him to remove them completely. I splayed my legs out as wide as I could.

He didn't need anything else. He slipped two fingers inside me at once since I was so drenched. *A low moan escaped my lips.*

My spouse inquired, *"Are you alright?"* He was glancing my way.

It's OK; *"I thought sitting on my son's lap would be an issue, but it truly is not."* I answered with a smile.

"It won't be too horrible," He says.

My son's fingers were embedded in my pussy as I spoke to my spouse.

"When are we going to come to an end of this road trip?"

He said, *"I don't want to stop until I'm a bit further down the road."*

I turned to my son in a soft voice,

"I'd want to see a little more from you, Joel."

Mom, you're right. As far as I'm concerned, *"I'm capable of much more."*

"That's good," I said.

"The more time we spend together, the more I enjoy it."

"Is it all right with you, honey?" My husband chimed in.

The thought of never stopping appeals to me. He responded.

To see my son's reaction, I spun around. *"As long as you keep going, I don't want to stop."*

"Joel?" my husband asked my son, *"How are you doing with your mom on your lap?"*

"No problem dad, mom keeps moving around so one position doesn't get uncomfortable. She raises up every once in a while to relieve the pressure."

As my son was talking to his dad, he was sinking his fingers even deeper in my pussy.

Joel's fingers were moving in and out of my wet pussy.

To prevent a groan, I bit my tongue. I put my hand on his shoulder. I pushed his hand hard into my pussy. That was something I wanted him to know. His fingers went deep into my pussy.

To the beat of his fingers, *I began swaying my hips.* My hubby was staring at me. It was fortunate that the television was in the way of his view. I don't know what he would do if he could see his son with his fingers buried in his mother's pussy.

My entire body was responding to his touch. He suddenly

yanked his fingers away from my pussy. I was let down.

That was short-lived. My son started taking the buttons off my shirt. He began to work his way down to the bottom button, starting at the top button.

At the same time, he was removing the buttons from my dress, I noticed how cool the car's air conditioner felt against my skin. My nipples were rendered even more sensitive by it. The last button was unbuttoned when I felt it. Afterward, he took the time to undress me.

My son could do whatever he wanted to me in front of my nude body. He began stroking my body with his hands. He began stroking my tits. He continued to hold them in his hands like that. I threw my chest out in order for him to push even harder on my tits.

It was time for me to come out from under my skirt. My youngster was able to deduce the reasoning behind this.

In order to unzip his shorts, he dropped both of his

hands. When he was unable to get to his zipper, I had to get up. I heard him unzipping his shorts. Still, I had his dick firmly lodged under my ass. My hips rose even higher.

Are you fine, honey? My spouse enquired, naturally.

"Are you having a hard time sitting on our son's lap?"

"Would you like me to slow down and park the car so you can relax?"

At the same time, Joel was taking his underwear off, and I could feel the tension building in his dick. Then I sat down on him again. He had his dick in my crotch and it was rubbing against my bare bottom.

I responded to my husband;

"Don't worry, honey, I guess I can make myself at home if I simply move around a little bit."

Then, I asked Joel;

"How are things going with you?

Is there anything else you require me to do so that you can feel relaxed?

Joel placed his hands on my hips, one on each side.

"Mom, if you'd just raise your head a bit so I can get a better position."

The words my son used made sense to me.

As high as I could, I raised my genitals into the air and held them there for a while. My hip felt a numbing sensation as one of his hands slipped off of it. It was clear to me what he was doing. I began to re-enter Joel's embrace. I was greeted by the head of his dick as soon as I was lowering my hip. I lowered my shoulders even further so that my husband won't know that I am undressed. He could only see my head slightly.

My pussy was simply slid into Joel's dick as I lower my hip further. The head of my son's dick was opening wide the opening of my pussy as I was lowering myself into it. I let out a low moan. That's what I ended up doing.

My husband gave me a sympathetic glance behind the wheel when he heard my sound, which was unknown to him that I was gently moaning.

"You don't want me to stop? Are you sure?" Asked, my husband.

As I lowered myself until I felt my son's dick bottom out in my pussy.

"No, no, don't stop, I want you to keep going. I'm good for the next half hour or so. What about you Joel, are you good for the next half hour? I said"

"Yeah mom, I made sure I was in a comfortable position before you sat back down on me."

For a brief moment, I must stand. *"Is that all right, Mom?"*

When it comes to rising up, do you want me to join you? I asked my son.

No. If you just stay on my lap, I positioned myself so

I would have no problem. My son responded by raising his hips and ramming his dick deeper into me while saying that. I was almost there at the time.

"It's time for me to settle in." When I moved my ass around, I made his penis go around inside of me even more. I caught a glimpse of my husband's face as I rode my son's dick.

Joel continued to exert maximum pressure on my pussy. Only if my husband knew. Here I am, bare-chested, fucking my son behind my spouse.

"How soon after Joel moves into his dorm do you think we can see him?" I asked my husband, just to engage him, and for him not to be suspicious.

My husband replied, *"You can go see him without me if you don't mind the drive because of my job schedule."*

I got even hungrier as I was talking to my husband while my son's dick was deep inside me. It's fine if you don't show up every time, and don't worry about it. The more I can make it to our son, the better.

That sounds OK right?

Joel responded; "*Mom, you're welcome to visit as often as you like.*" I think it'll be even better if more of you come.

When he was done talking, he shoved me hard. He whispered to my ears, "How soon do you suppose you'll cum?"

"Really soon, Joel," I said

I began swiping my ass against his crotch. My only moving part was my groin. In order to keep my spouse from figuring out what we were doing, I kept my head immobile.

An orgasm was imminent. When Joel's hands were no longer on my hips, I put them on my tits. It was too much for me to take when my son put his hands on my tits. I was slammed by wave after wave as they rolled over me. I was unable to do anything but stiffen my muscles.

Approximately thirty seconds elapsed between. One

of my best and most satisfying orgasms. I sank into my son's arms, exhausted.

My experience with Joel wasn't over yet. He kept shoving his genitalia into my crotch (He kept thrusting his dick in me). His legs sprang out in front of him. My son began firing his cum deep inside me. It was energizing for me. It was quite cozy. Until he emptied me of his cum, I remained still. Both of us were exhausted by the experience.

A notice (Billboard) says an eatery can be found about 10 miles down the road.

Do you guys mind? My husband asked.

Joel answered, "*Yeah, Dad, I could eat something.*" I turned around to see Joel staring back at me. The man was beaming at me. I'm curious about your thoughts, Mom. Is there anything you'd want to eat?

A hot dog or anything might do the trick for me, but I'm quite full.

I went down to pick up my pants that had fallen on

the car's floor mat. My son's dick fell out of me as I bent over to pick them up. I pulled up the panties with my feet, which I inserted into the pants' legs. Before, I dragged them over my pussy and slapped them on. My son got horny again, he went and stuck his finger in me again. I gave him a playful slap on his hand. He took his finger out of me and I pulled my panties up. I started buttoning up my dress. He put his dick back in his pants and zipped up.

I asked my husband a question; *"After dinner, how far are we from our destination?"*

My husband chimed in. "It would take around two and a half hours."

Do you guys think you can manage that?"

"I'm not going to complain, I can cope," I assured my husband.

"I'll sit on Joel's lap for another two hours if he'll have me."

Then, Joel, how are things going with you, and would you be able to cope with me sitting on your lap for the next 2 hours? I asked"

"I thought the first two hours passed by rather quickly, too. As fast as or perhaps faster, I expect the following two hours to go likewise. Joel responded"

"I was expecting at least one of you to voice your displeasure by now," My husband said.

"Are there any issues that you'd like to raise son?" I asked Joel after telling my husband I had no displeasure"

"Mom, even if the ride went on forever, I wouldn't complain," Joel said.

The next two hours are going to be fantastic for you I promise he said.

Thank you, son, I can't wait to experience another 2 hours ride on your lap at the back seat.

…Continue to chapter 2

Check out the continuation of this story in the next chapter.

Chapter 2

Road Trip Continuation

"Well, sweetie, there should be hot dogs here." What do you think? My Dad asked.

Is this a place where we can eat? What is the bus stop's name? Dad inquired as he parked the automobile.

"No problem honey... hot dog is excellent any time of the day... huh Joel?"

As she looked up at me, Mom tried to mask the dangerous, panting lilt in her voice by feigning a yawn and smiling.

As I thrust back, she was still sitting on my lap, rubbing her hefty, meaty ass against my crotch with my hands on her hips.

Mother: "Ugh... yeah?" I let out a groan. My dad might have misunderstood my gasp of pleasure as a positive response to her question.

As we resumed our dry humping, the only barriers between us were her flimsy summer dress and panties and my shorts and boxers. I was trying to enjoy the ride as much as possible before we had to stop soon.

When it was 10 miles away, it was a completely different story.

Innocently enough, the day began.

Dad, Mom, and I finally finished packing our car to the brim with all of my belongings for college, which was five hours away on a scorching late August afternoon (nearing midday).

When I noticed at the last minute that my enormous flat-screen TV had been left out of the packing, I insisted on moving everything else to make room for it. When I insisted on bringing that electronic device, I didn't anticipate that it would lead to an all-day ride with my lovely, mature mom.

She had given birth to me (her only child) at the age

of 19, and despite the passage of time, she still appeared to be in her prime. Mom had curly, shoulder-length, dark brown hair and wide, brown eyes with naturally long lashes.

She was small, perhaps 5 feet tall. She has a striking resemblance to *Martha Harper* from the television program **"Weeds,"** but in my opinion, she is more attractive and has a more appealing facial beauty.

Even a few hours ago, I wasn't thinking about these things because our journey had been delayed by Mom's insistence that we all take another shower before we left, and I was a little irritated by her. The day was hot, and we were all sweating from transporting and packing all of my belongings, so I didn't see the sense in continuing the conversation.

It was only when we were ready to go that I realized how cramped the front seat was, with my 42-inch TV occupying much of the space that Mom and I could fit.

Dad and I were the first to hop in. When he saw me,

barely able to see above the TV, he inquired whether Mom and I were okay (it was turned sideways with the screen facing my side of the car). The only thing that bothered her was whether or not Dad would be able to drive, so she crammed herself into my lap and insisted she was alright.

At last, we were on our way, and I found myself looking sideways in the rear-view mirror, saying my final goodbyes to the places I had called home for the previous 20 years.

I didn't notice her until we were on the road for about twenty minutes when she sat on my crotch with her smooth, naked legs brushing mine. As recently as a week ago, I was thinking about my ex-girlfriend, with whom I had broken up because she had decided that we should just part ways peacefully because she was moving to a different college. When I realized that this was my mother's warm, gorgeous butt pressing firmly on my penis and pent-up balls with only a few pieces of clothing in between, I felt conflicted about possibly never seeing her again and frustrated about not having had any pussy in the last few months.

To my horror, *I was becoming a boner as a result of my repressed lust! My erection was responding to the unanticipated feminine stimulation produced by Mom's ass, so she must have felt the sprouting log of my erection.*

I attempted to distract myself from the embarrassing situation by listening to the radio, but it didn't work.

My hands accidentally brushed against Mom's bare thighs as I became a little dizzy and couldn't find anything else to hold on to. I noticed that Mom's dress and skirt had ridden up as she started fidgeting a little.

At first, she just asked if I was okay, but as her writhing around on top of me became more rhythmic, I realized how much she must have been enjoying it.

She put her hands firmly on her thighs after grabbing mine. In the end, all I needed was consent from her to give in to nature's impulses, and that was given to me by her sly grin and the glazed expression in her eyes as she fluttered her lashes up at me. We were all dry humping!

From there, things only got better. *Even though we occasionally peeked over the TV at Dad as he drove to make absolutely sure he didn't notice what we were doing, we grew more daring in our prohibited amusements with time.*

When Mom invited me to finger her wet pussy when her pants were down to her knees, I was shocked. She started a conversation with my father about how long the trip was and how she was feeling. Mom's dress was unbuttoning and I was tickling her plump tits and having my way with her body while I agreed with him that we were good.

Even though we had another hour or so of driving ahead of us before we were likely to stop for lunch, I knew I had to push my big dick in Mom and fuck her as good as I can possibly do.

I had no idea if this opportunity would ever come

my way again. A few feet away, Mom and Dad were engaged in a raunchy double-sided conversation, and I, too, was eager to join in, hoping to ratchet up the sexiness so that both of us would be able to satisfy our sexual desires.

She offered me the opportunity to liberate my aching big dick rapidly as she permitted me to make an excuse to swap positions. Her panties slipped from her knees to the floor when she elevated her ass just a tad too high. **JACKPOT!**

I swiftly dragged her back down as her hot, spread buttocks looked inviting. This time, I finally got her to allow me to enter her inviting tightness, but it took some time and further tweaks.

In one fast shove, I was able to easily slide my cockhead and veiny shaft inside Mom's damp, sticky vaginal. When I hit rock bottom, Mom let out a cute, horny groan (distractingly drowned out by the radio) and I smirked as she chatted with my ignorant Dad.

We were in a frenetic, tumultuous, taboo fuck, and Mom was an expert at disguising her words with double meaning. She even got me involved.

It was at this point that her words became too much for us both, and she screamed all over my big cock while I was burying myself to the balls in her and blasting her vagina full of cum. The force of my climax ejaculation had both of my legs frozen straight out. When I spastically jerked my legs, ropes of hot, healthy sperm were released into her vagina with each jerk. This made all of the anxiety and aggravation from the previous months and the previous weeks seem to go away.

Mum sat calmly while I drained 5 months' worth of rage into her — her hot ass squelching my whirling nuts.

With her twitch, she managed to coax every last ounce of passion from me. At one point, while the cum-shot continued to fire, I could feel her cervix lapping squarely against my cock tip.

Her most sacred spot, the place where babies are

born, was being invaded by thick white wads of my potent, youthful gunk, which contained my energetic genetic messengers.

My hot, 20-year-old cock made me understand my mother was still only 39 and could definitely still get pregnant, but at the time, I didn't give a fuck. Having a condom on hand was the last thing on my mind when I packed my bags today.

Hopefully, she was on the pill. Regardless, I'd fuck her again as soon as I could. Even a small part of me wished that I had knocked her unconscious. My small, little swimmers meeting her egg; our DNA combining; Mom conceiving and giving birth while I was away at college; then making Dad assist in raising my child, thinking it was his — it was all so dirty, perverted, and nasty!

I was disgusted! During the time Mom was on my chest, I wondered how big her clammy tits would get as I kneaded them with my fingers. That my cock milk could be directly responsible for her jugs producing milk made me chuckle.

Mom and I were exhausted as we came to terms with our post-orgasmic euphoria.

Mercifully, we hadn't made it to Dad's planned lunch break at the rest area when we put our clothes back on. While it was still a few miles away, Mom and I were able to get in a bit more fun. Before we stopped, my hard-on had returned, and I wanted to spend as much time as possible with her hot a** before it went away.

After Dad's abrupt question about the breakfast cafe, we were unable to continue our playful adventure any longer.

We arrived at the restaurant, and Mom and I were forced to put an end to our merrymaking. Before she sat down slowly on me, she lifted herself up a bit and quickly straightened out her skirt, perhaps so Dad wouldn't notice. Personally, I had to find some way of getting rid of the fresh hard-on in my shorts before we were allowed to step out of the vehicle. Mom flashed me a wink when she realized I was in trouble (in more ways than one) due to my erection.

"Uh... honey? Surely Joel can go back there and check on his belongings to see if anything has changed, don't you think? " She told my Dad.

"It's definitely a sport." Then he handed me the keys while he turned off the car's engine.

After both of them emerged, *I took a few moments to admire the view of her ass that had been riding me (and I'd been pounding her) for the last few hours.*

That hard thing wasn't going to go away easily, so I'm delighted Mom came up with this plan to help me calm down.

After what felt like an eternity, I was finally able to leave after only a few seconds. To pass the time, I feigned to tie my shoelaces and then kept reaching back and pretending to check on my other belongings.

Yes, my baby's favorite TV is OK. As soon as I got

outside, Mom began to torment me.

"Yes, Ma'am," I reply. I laughed and rolled my eyes back at her.

Her hair was being styled, and Dad was extending his legs next to her.

It's a wonderful concept, honey! Mom uttered the words, then lowered her head and reached for her feet.

Prior to the next two-hour ride on top of our young son, *"You gotta stretch while You can!"* Said my Dad.

My mom smiled sexily, fluttering her eyelids, and she giggled back.

Squats were not something she had ever done before, so she carefully bounced her large rear a couple times like she was doing them. Reluctantly, I turned away after realizing that this was doing more harm than good to my lower body.

I went to the back of the car and opened the hatch,

deliberately shifting a few items and stalling. Taking a pair of basketball shorts from a bag and slinging them over my shoulder, I headed out the door. In high school, I used to have one of these, and I remembered how well the breathable mesh fabric worked for me when I was on a state-qualifying team. Wickedly, I wondered if it would be useful in the future for a few other things. I guess you understand what I mean. *Wink*

I've got to go pee now. Keep in mind that we still have at least two and a half to three hours of driving ahead of us. With that, Dad stormed inside the restaurant like a bull.

My mother walked up to me slowly after making sure he was no longer there.

She smooched me sexily as she snatched her purse from the trunk, noting my basketball shorts.

"Well, sort of?" *"But seriously, Mom, it's freaking hot out here,"* I said meekly. Simply put, I want something *"cooler."*

She slapped my butt as she giggled, saying, *"Something easier to get off like it right?"*

In the words of my Mom, *"Joel, you are a silly boy!"*

When Mom called me by my name, I assumed something had gone horribly wrong, but the light-hearted tone in her voice as she laughed made me feel better.

To ensure our safety, Mom hopped in the car to kiss me in the middle of the back seat with her tiptoed heel.

You were *"extremely bad"* for fiddling with your mother in such a way, but Mom liked it! As she cooed, she nibbled my lobe and kissed me on the cheek.

She gasped and collapsed into my arms as I yanked her closer to me with lusty jerks.

You're not allowed to be out here, young man! She reprimanded me in a mocking manner, her finger pointing at me.

Joel, hurry up and have your slacks changed. We still have a long way to go, just like your father said. "

My increasing bulging penis was gently caressed, with her emphasis on the term "*looooong*" as she did so.

Mom, if you don't leave me alone, I'll never be able to get comfortable! No worries, I'll smack you in between now.

As I bent down to reach inside her skirt and fondled her juicy pussy, stressing "*I'll be right in there...*"

When I tried to get closer to Mom's slit, she quickly twisted away, smacking my palm away in amusement.

What a scoundrel of a son! She said, "*What would you like Mommy to get for you?*"

Whatever my dad is eating is fine with me. The final time, I held Mom by the waist and said, "*... like maybe his wife!*" She nodded in agreement.

I gave her a cheeky squeeze through her skirt, then sent her out with a final slap of her rump.

As we parted ways, we both gave each other a philandering smile.

In my basketball shorts (which were both cooler and less restricting), I headed to the restaurant to get some food.

As was their tradition, Mom and Dad sat across from one another and chatted happily as they ate their "breakfast for supper."

Finally! Take action now, Joel. When we served you pancakes, we weren't sure if you wanted anything extra, so we prepared a plate for you. *"Here, have a seat beside me!"*

We both sat down, and Mom patted the seat in front of us. She only had bread, a little salad, and some fruit and juice on her plate.

Besides the pancakes, bacon, and sausage, he also had a cup of coffee. My father, who is approaching

50 and has a receding hairline, needs to pay more attention to what he eats.

Mom, this is fine. All of that fried food is out of the question for me. For the coach's tryouts next month, I need to keep my basketball shape.

It's not important, so don't worry about it. " As a matter of fact, honey, a young person requires a lot of carbohydrates. He'll have to haul all that stuff afterward, you know, young man! Dad slapped his son's leg with an irritating cackle.

Even if I wanted to smirk or "accidentally" kick him in the shins right then and there, I couldn't help myself.

Joel, don't listen to your father. She reached under the table and secretly pinched my nuts through my shorts while saying this without anybody else in the dining room knowing what she was doing.

Her actions made it difficult not to groan.

I'm really sorry. I forgot to bring my basketballs with

me.

"Mom, would it be okay if you brought them over next week?"

"Of course, my son."

Just hold on to them till then, okay? Mom smiled as she massaged my balls under the table.

Upon my arrival to join them in the diner, I wondered,

"So, what were you two talking about when I arrived?" As I tucked into my pancakes," I inquired.

After getting back on the road, I was ready to eat the dinner so I could serve it up to Fucking Mom once again.

"Oh, no worries, I'll be back in no time!" *"…and visit you!"* was a risky pause.

You know, assist you with settling into your residence hall. She said to me.

"Next weekend would be ideal," I said.

Mom's gorgeous brown lashes fluttered as she smiled at me.

When Mom blinked her clandestine invitation for more incestuous sex, it was as if we were using a secret telegraphic code.

I can't wait to see you, Mom, next week! I'd definitely appreciate your help in unloading...

"In order to give her time to digest that period of silence, I purposefully popped some pancakes into my mouth. Meanwhile, I was fantasizing about fucking Mom's brains out all next weekend and unloading my balls on her. Unloading my belongings and organizing them was what I'm talking about openly, as opposed to what my real plans were in my mind."

Grinning back at her, I returned the lusty stare that had been exchanged between us without words. We were lost in thought.

"September is the busiest month of the year for my job, and I can't join you and your mother on the trip because I'll be too busy at work," Dad interjected.

You're welcome, Dad. In my dorm, Mom and I will be fine. (Fine while we fuck freely!) I sneered at my own thoughts.

Mom was the first to finish her light dinner and make her way to the women's bathroom to "freshen up," whatever that meant.

Having eaten most of what was in front of me, I was eager to resume our journey, but Dad was taking his sweet time.

When Mom came out of the bathroom, he was chewing on a toothpick and had finished his meal. There was something strange about her, but I couldn't place what it was at the time (later pun intended).

Do you think one plate of pancakes was sufficient for you, sportsman?

"Is there anything more we should buy for the trip? The sun will fall soon, and we're only halfway to your school, so I don't want to stop for food again," Dad said.

As soon as he got outside, he lit up a foul-smelling cigar.

The answer is *"yes,"* I said.

Don't pretend that you won't get hungry after a few hours. It's got to be the youthful vigor and metabolism, right?

"Go with your father to the car; I'll place another order with the waitress for more food." Mom hurriedly closed the little purse after retrieving her wallet.

With a *"whatever,"* I shook my head and made my way out the door.

"Come over Joel!" So; I did a brief twirl and returned to her.

"Be a sweetheart and put Mommy's purse back in the trunk," she instructed. She dragged me back when I

was about to leave the room.

"If you take the time to look around, you may be in for a pleasant surprise," she said, her voice hushed.

That grabbed my interest.

After one last tug, she peered up into my eyes and then down at my crotch suggestively.

When I get back, I want to make sure you're all *"settled in,"* she mewed, one of her fingers just touching the waistband of my shorts, pulling at it a little.

I dashed outside to our car as fast as I could, more so to avoid popping a boner in the middle of that diner in front of everyone's eyes.

So; when I went to put Mom's purse away in the trunk, I immediately snapped the lid off to see what "surprise" she had in store for me.

What I witnessed had me in a state of awe -- In the purse she had been carrying around, white cotton pants were found. She was completely bare naked beneath her summer dress at this moment. Upon closer inspection, I discovered a wet spot in the crotch caused by our mixed juices—her cream and my seed—leaking from her cunt.

In the blink of an eye, I had a hardon.

A few minutes later, it dawned on me what Mom's subtle change in demeanor was...

It wouldn't be long before I was putting more than just my fingers on that! That's more like my fat crotch!

I returned to my seat at the back of the car and waited impatiently for Dad to finish smoking his cigar and for Mom to return. It's possible the cigar could be a blessing in disguise; it might mask some of the odors.

I nervously pushed my fingers into my waistband and lowered my basketball shorts to my ankles, remembering Mom's earlier order to *"settle"* myself in. No one outside could see this eager 20-year-old sitting in the back seat of our car with a rude erection tenting high and tall from his crotch because of our car's tinted side windows.

After finishing his cigar, Dad got in the car and heated it up. No doubt about it, the smell of the cigar would mask some of the odors. After what seemed like an eternity, Mom emerged with a white paper bag containing the food.

"Oh!" As she opened the door to the car, Mom said something to me. She rapidly handed the bag to me and slipped back into my lap before anyone else could see her.

The two of you can get settled in, but let me know when you're ready to go." As he fumbled with the wipers and headlights, Dad said. (He had no idea of what was happening.)

I adjusted the seat backwards to make a little more room for the bag. She grabbed her short skirt's hem as I lifted her up by her thighs. My hands followed hers and subsequently rested atop hers as I lowered her bare ass onto my throbbing cock in slow motion.

Both of us sighed with pleasure as my hard, naked dick made contact with her smooth, soft behind for the second time in a row. Fortunately, the radio was back on, and Dad didn't hear a peep.

After a few squirms of her cute little butt, Mom allowed me to get a good grip of her delicious rear end with my veiny shaft.

"We're good to go now, dear... The sun will set soon, and you know how terrible your eyesight is in the dark. Don't hurry to reach our destination. "

That part of my life is still ahead of me, you know. Dad took a deep breath and huffed.

Remember, we've got all the time in the world, dear... "Just remember, dear..." Mom paused, then went silent.

Finally, we were on our way again as dusk fell, the sun beginning to set over our heads in the west as we made our way through the countryside. As Mom writhed forward and backward on top of me, my raging erection still rubbed against the crack in her hot, bubbly ass. It wasn't until a few miles into the ride that I realized how much I was missing out on the pleasurable sensation of the rubbing between my shaft and Mom's butt.

When she got into it, she really got into it, thrusting her wide hips up and down, with each upward thrust, my engorged member rising ever higher. In the end, I shifted slightly on one of her up-thrusts and fissured it astoundingly along the lips of her slowly creaming wet pussy as my dick approached heaven.

As Mom's slick slash slathered my cock with the first layer of her honeydew, we both let out a soft, breathy moan. Oh, how I want to re-enter her cozy confines and plow her under once more!

Even though I was out of her pussy, my mother kept me entertained by gently stroking the length of my shaft with her fingers, peeking into my privates to check on how much sweat had collected on the top of my sperm-filled balls, and stroking my cock's head as she purred softly in my ear. Her sweet, tight pussy was all I could think about, and I couldn't wait to scoop it up and unload another thick stack into her womb.

Even as the minutes and miles ticked by, Mom's taunts managed to keep me at bay. But don't get me wrong, I was greatly entertained by her eroticism.

She was driving me crazy! A long time had passed, yet Mom's enticing words had eluded my achy tool for all that time. If I didn't pounce on her as we both knew she needed, would she just let me go?

After leaving the dinner, the fact that no one had spoken to us since then made us uneasy, aside from the radio music. Damn it! That wasn't an option for me.

"How long are you going to keep torturing me?" I whispered in her ear.

Her grin spread across her face as she replied,

"You've got to show me you're hungry enough, Joel."

What on earth did you mean by that?

Mom handed me the bag of food from the restaurant as if she had read my thoughts because she reached down and casually picked it up. I was still perplexed as to what she was trying to say. Looking inside, I couldn't figure out why I was so perplexed. In addition to some bread, there were several Styrofoam containers with large sausages, scrambled eggs in one, and a container of some white stuff — probably gravy. I handed the bag back to Mom because I didn't understand why it was so important to me. Exasperatedly, she rolled her eyes at me.

You're starving, aren't you, Joel?

It was shocking to hear a normal-volume voice after so many miles of silence (*aside from Mom and my whispered messages to her*). It appeared as if Mom was overstating her voice.

"Yes, of course, Mom. What's in there, then?"

I went along with it, even though I had no idea what was going on. We were continuing grinding, but suddenly it stopped when Mom raised her ass to get up, and then made a point of audibly rummaging through the paper bag.

What am I going to do?

"I've got these buns. They look great, don't they?" I asked her, with a childlike tone of voice.

As she returned with the dinner rolls, she gave them to me with a smile. Despite my confusion, I held them up to my face and looked at them. A few seconds ago, I was about to bite into one.

What do you think of these BUNS, Joel? Mom went over it again and again.

My attention switched from the bread to the obvious wriggling inches in front of me that I had missed. What the hell is going on?

Her skirt was cinched at the waist, exposing her ass while her hips moved sensually back and forth.

When she spread her buns apart, she did it with both hands on her buttocks.

Those hairs! The realization of it all came to me more like a flash of lightning.

Mom, you're right. *"Then I'll get a taste of that! "*

"That's OK, son. Dive right in! "

It was with my hands on her hips that I brought her down hard to my crotch. My mother extended a helping hand and lifted my stiff cock to meet her gaze. Touchdown! with a single horny thrust. My mother's clammy, pussy-clutching lips were punctured by my cockhead and shaft, and I was completely submerged in her cunt.

After she was snugly nestled in my balls, I slowly raised her up and lowered her slowly back down. After that, it was time for some more ball-busting fun, and I was in heaven!

The best buns you've ever had, Mom! *Mmmmmrrrgh...* Grumbling, I pretended to be eating.

That's right, son. I'm aware of the situation. You'd like some more of this?

Smacking her lips, Mom replied.

My shaft was soon covered in Mom's juices as we sped up. To further enjoy the tightness of her succulent pussy, I squeezed her hips even tighter. Her ample butt was just the right height for me to eagerly thrust up into, and our pacing and timing were perfect. I could feel my hard cock back in heaven.

"Ha! Are you two still peckish? I knew you should have stuffed yourself at the dinner. Maybe I should stop driving for you both to stretch a bit?"

When he interrupted our filthy fuck, Dad's voice was loud and grating.

No, please don't! My mom said.

Joel, *"are you sure you don't want to stop? "* Her voice was a little shaky.

"No..."

My Mom said, we've got a long way to go... We can manage to stretch and readjust ourselves in the car. We don't need to stop until we get to the school."

That's all right, you two. Then carry on.

Honey, *"please don't make a mess in the car with you and your son about hunger! "* My dad said

We smiled at each other as we looked at each other. When she clambered forward, she drew out the container with the sausages and set it down on the counter. I was the first to reach for a fork and take a bite.

Mom, *"What about a bit of my sausage? "*

Mmmm...

Put it on my thighs, Joel! Your sausage is a lot more robust than the wrinkly one your father used to eat! " (She whispered to my ears).

"Mom, I know!"

We exchanged passionate kisses as we smacked our lips together. Then I really started giving it to her. Double-talking and putting one over on Dad were taken to a whole new level in this charade, and I was savoring every moment of it.

The pussy-lip-smacking and the constant "schluck! schluck! schluck!" of our unhurried and joyful forbidden fucking carried on for what seemed like an eternity, our false eating sensations helping to disguise the actual cause.

We didn't eat any of the pretend food because it was too gross, but I have to confess that the calories from the food did assist Mom and I continue our casual, illegal encounters.

The Eagles' *Witchy Woman* was screaming on the radio. Mom whispered in my ear as we were about 30 minutes from my college.

"It's time for you to take the final course."

The following container was pulled from my purse

by my hand. We kept up our feigned suckling. My cock kept on banging Mom's pussy from the bottom.

It's time for some more of that, son! My mother's whine was loud and desperate.

My genitals did as she asked and stepped up the tempo. It became more obvious that I would not be able to withstand the growing pains of my rumbling balls.

Your son, dear, is disobeying. "Tell him to give some eggs to his mother! " Mom told Dad.

"Pay attention to what Mom says, sportsman." Dad said.

"Are you absolutely certain, Dad?" I asked Dad.

"Danggit! Your mother will appreciate some scrambled eggs from you, son."

"That's fine, Papa!"

Suddenly, I accelerated my thrust to an ecstatic rate. As we neared our climax, Mom kept up with me, bouncing her plump, moist ass, meeting me stroke for stroke. The words I wanted to scream were ringing out in my head as I sat inches from my father:

"All right, Dad!" I'll cook Mom's egg for her. Her egg should be scrambled with MY SEED!!

What if I mixed her genes with my own?

*THERE'S A BABY IN HER!!! I'M CREATING A CHILD IN HER!!! Those youthful, loaded balls will be shot dry of sperm before I put a baby up for adoption. Your dear wife, my mom! "**"*

As soon as I felt the usual tingle and pang in my heavy, clenched nuts, I knew I had to take action. I could already tell this was going to be a heavy load when I got this close!

Joel, that's so good! That sack's bottom could be a little too far for you, son. "

"Yeah, Mom!" exclaimed Mom.

" *Mom?"* I blurted out. My mind was racing.

You can count on me to go deep into my nutsack for

you, Mom!

*You can count on me to go deep into my nutsack for you, Mom! 'That includes reaching deep inside of YOU! Millions of my Joel will be shot directly into your belly if you let me reach deep within you! If I can't go deep inside you and knock you up with my f*cking baby, DAD has NO IDEA HOW TO STOP IT!!! "** (Joel whispered)*

When I retrieved the container of white gravy, I chuckled once more at Mom's cleverness. There was nothing she hadn't considered.

"Mom, what are you going to do with this white stuff?"

"Joel, just get rid of it. I'd want some of that white, hot gravy on my eggs! Give me as much as you can!"

It's fine, Mom!

So that was it. It took Mom's final comments to pique my lustful curiosity about everything's obscene double meaning.

Then, with one final frenzied thrust, I was back in Mom's clutching cunt, my balls deep in the dirt. Mom's cervix was brutally penetrated by my pre-cum leaking cockhead as the first searing string of semen shot from my piss-hole in a single second. Staggering amounts of baby-batter, all of which came straight to Mom, down her womb.

"Uuuuuuuuuuuuuuuuuuuuuuuuuu, Joel, you're leaking it all over the place! " Mom shrieked with delight.

That's certainly what I was thinking. My seed was strewn all over my mother. embedded in her were mounds of my ancestry. Even though I was exhausted, I continued going. Young adult sperm streamed into Mom's unprotected, receptive, and welcoming womb, one wad at a time.

Sorry, Mom, it's just so much! But, oh my gosh, it's so good, huh? " It made me want to throw up, and I moaned.

I made noises as if I was sucking my fingers, but what I was actually doing was sucking on one of Mom's firm nipples.

Mom was cuddling with me, and I realized it when I felt something warm dripping over my genitals. As I continued to push myself into her creaming fuckwit, her pussy would squirt her own delightful, feminine honey all over my penis. Stirring our raging stew of sexy, steamy, and hormone-fueled sludge, I bit into my lip and stirred. A bubbling brew was made when my mother and I mixed our banned, FAMILIAL Fuck-froth.

You are stirring it up so much! "Oh.. Joel, you are stirring it so much!!!"

"Danggit! It's awful, right? " Dad just kind of spewed it out.

"Nnnnngh... The majority of your son's white material got into my container, dear..."

You don't have to worry, Dad! Mom's package contained all of my gravy! "

There is no harm in giving your mother a second helping

if she's still hungry.

Mmmmmmm, ahhhhhhhh, that's fine.

"Yes," Joel, "Gimme some more of that gravy, sweetheart!"

'There you have it, *Mommmmmm!*'

Mom and I sighed softly after a full dinner as we indulged our primitive needs while also obediently honoring Dad's stupid instruction.

With the help of her pussy, my mother was able to extract every last drop from my genitals. I could feel Mom's squirming cervix slurping up my sperm like it was her own, and I was mortified. All of my possessions were eagerly given to her. As much of my swarming, swimming genetic gunk as I could get into Mom, in her hallowed womb, where kids are conceived, was my goal for this mission in life.

In order to discover her egg for as long as I could, I would send every last thrashing packet of DNA that my testicles could produce out into the world. It would be nice if Mom's ovaries helped out. The one thing I longed for more than anything else was the chance for one of my lucky baby-makers *(out of the countless millions I was giving Mom right then and there)* to meet Mom's ovum. Mother Nature would take care of the rest, ensuring that Mom would be knocked up in the process.

If he's done, make sure you acquire all of his belongings! I told you not to mess up, son! "

Don't worry, sweetheart! I've got it all covered. "

"Dad, I couldn't have done it!" I laughed cruelly to myself as I smiled.

Relishing in the sweet satisfaction of post-orgasmic adrenaline and youthful testosterone, my body was tingling with excitement. When I realized that I had once again crammed Mom's fridge to the brim, I felt like I had won the lottery.

As a bonus, I had the illicit thrill of knowing that Mom had been my consenting partner, knowingly putting one of my 20-year-old sperm inside of her 39-year-old Mommy eggs to meet. The prospect of becoming incestuously pregnant by me, her own son, seemed to excite her to no end. This all happened just inches away from her husband, my dad, who was completely unaware (or ignorant) of it all!

As we neared the college town's outskirts, I finally popped my satisfied penis out of Mom's ravished cunt. While peering into Mom's crotch, I was pleasantly surprised to find a minimal amount of slobber. The majority of my ammo must have been fired into her at the precise location I had in mind.

Despite the fact that Mom's skirt drooped down to her knees, she quickly straightened her skirt and pulled her thighs together. Smiling softly, she put her feet on the foot mat while crossing her calves and falling into me. My heart warmed when my eyes met hers and she smiled back at me. After that, I had peace of mind knowing my awesome deposit was secure!

My arms were wrapped around Mom's abdomen as I sat back and relaxed. I smiled wryly at seeing Mom raised on her elbows. Now that she'd provided them with some gravitational assistance, I wondered how my squirming mass of teenager-sized larvae were doing in her twat. After a while of lying like that, Mom got up and started cleaning off some of the crumbs and other debris that had accumulated in the back seat. My semi-hard cannon was a little unhappy to be put away as I put my basketball shorts back on.

My mom slid the window down, allowing us to breathe in some cool, refreshing late-summer air. We were both relieved when the thin film of post-fuck sweat that had been covering us vanished. Something else, of course, was scattered to the winds. I realize now that most of the car's lingering odor was caused by Dad's stinky cigar.

We got to my dorm just before 7 p.m. When we arrived, Mom was the first to get out of the car and dashed to the trunk to find her pants. Dad and I had just finished stretching when I noticed her dash to the restroom (I grinned to myself, knowing the true reason why).

After Mom returned, we began loading up my belongings, starting with my big-screen TV, which had been the source of my day-long fling with her earlier in the day.

When my belongings were finally unloaded from the car and delivered to my room, it was far past 9 p.m. As a result, I felt confident that I would still be able to spend the weekend with Mom alone.

The three of us made it back to the car together.

"Oh my gosh, how time flies by! My beautiful baby will be sorely missed."

As we prepared to say goodbye, Mom squealed and cradled me in her arms.

"Don't worry, my dear. Someday, they'll all have to leave

the nest and grow. And don't forget that you'll see him again next weekend to assist him with unloading. " My father comforted her.

Make sure to pack his basketballs, too, honey. Perhaps you and your mother could play a game of basketball next week, eh? "

"Hmmmmm... I'm stumped, my dear! A one-on-one meeting between your boy and his mother would be a good test. " Mom made a sly remark.

"Ah! I'm sure he'd shoot you all over the place! " Dad snorted and laughed.

My mother and I exchanged a sly grin.

My heart was full of joy as she came back to me and said, *"I love you."*

How about a little *"sport"*, or should I say *"young stud"*?

"Are you interested in continuing your father's wager? Mommy's basket with her other balls might be more fun,

though!"

I couldn't help but smile.

Mom returned to Dad's side, tugging on his arm with her free hand.

Do you think we might be able to have another child in the future? You DO realize how young I am? "

Ah! then What in the world did you come up with? As soon as our first child starts college, you're already talking about having another one! Besides, do you still take security measures? "

While Dad was shaking my hand firmly to say goodbye, Mom had a wicked grin on her face. She then returned my hypnotic glance.

As soon as I saw it, I recognized it.

"No, dear, I haven't been taking the pill for a while now."

Check out the third book in this series Our Secret (Mother and Son's Secret Book 3) to read about how Joel fantasy grew bigger by fucking his mom, and also his aunt in the next chapter.

Chapter 3

Our Secret

Tasha, his mother's younger sister, arrived at the house bright and early on Saturday morning.

"Hi squirt," she said. Joel didn't resent the slam; it was a nickname she had given him when he was born.

At the time, she was eight and thought the name was cute. They had always been closer than most nephews and aunts, and with a typical little girl's thought process, she felt it was her duty to help take care of him.

"Hi, Tasha," Ellen and Joel said in unison. "What's up?" his mother (Ellen) added.

Don't you two remember, you promised to help me take some furniture out to the storage shed at Mom and Dad's farm?

Oh, I completely forgot, but it doesn't matter because

it's all separated in the back bedroom. She turned to her son. "Can you help Joel?"

"Yeah," he agreed. I've got nothing planned for the day. Sam's out of town and Jeff is sick in bed, so there's no one to hang out with."

As husky as Joel was, it was still a lot of work to load the bed, chest, and boxes from their house into the pickup. They began loading the pickup truck with those furniture and boxes.

Finally, after two hours, they were ready to go. Joel covered the load because it looked like it was going to rain, and even had to move a couple of the boxes inside the truck, setting them on the seat behind Tasha.

"You're going to have to sit on Joel's lap," Tasha said to Ellen. As she was to drive the truck "There won't be enough room to sit because of these boxes, and other loads."

That will be alright, won't it Joel?" his mother said.

"Well, as long as you don't weigh a ton and take up the whole side of the truck," he said, laughing.

"I'll have you know I weigh one hundred pounds, young man, and I'm only five foot tall, not six foot three." She was grinning when she said it, but there was a little bit of pride in her voice.

At thirty-nine, his mother had the body and looks of a high school senior. Although few high school girls had 36C boobs that were full, firm, and had such prominent nipples, plus a number ten ass.

Calling his attention to her body was not the best thing she could have done.

He settled himself in the seat and she hopped in and, placing her feet between his, she lowered herself to his lap.

She was wearing a thin summer dress, and he had seen only a bikini panty line and a bra under it. He immediately felt the heat from her body flow into his crotch area.

He turned his mind to the road ahead.

Tasha pulled away, and moments later they were on the country road to the farm, twenty miles away.

The road was under construction for more than five miles, and the truck bounced with a steady rhythm as it rolled along the ridges left by the road grader.

Tasha and Ellen kept up a constant chat about women things, leaving Joel with his own thoughts.

In time, he became aware of the rhythmic bouncing and the heat coming from his mother's ass as it pressed against his crotch, which made him feel hot.

Suddenly, to his horror, his cock began responding to the movement. He felt the first stirrings of a hard-on. He tried to think of other things, but the more he tried thinking of other things, the more he thought of his cock.

Gradually, his dick became firmer and began to rise, until it was contained by the ass pressing down on it. This pressure only succeeded in causing it to become more rigid until it was like a bar of steel. He could feel the crack between his mother's legs, and finally, her pussy, as the rigid shaft forced itself against the spread lips of her ass.

There was no doubt she could feel the hard bar against her panty-covered ass, but she made no motion or comment that indicated she was aware of his predicament.

Ellen first ignored the hard rod pushing against her ass. Then, without thinking, she adjusted herself slightly and the pressure switched directly to her pussy.

In the beginning, she was irritated that her own son would get an erection from her sitting on his lap. But the more she thought about it, the funnier it became.

What a waste of a good hard-on she thought; getting rigid for your mother. Ellen almost laughed out loud. The bouncing of the seat, caused the hard member to slip back and forth along her ass.

Then a sudden bump drove his cock head against her, forcing her panties and thin dress between her thigh for just a split second.

A minute later, thinking about the incident, Ellen realized that technically, for that split second, her son's cock had been touching her pussy.

True, it had just been the very tip and it had been covered by panties and a dress, but was that any different than being covered by a condom?

The thought was so erotic, that her pussy flooded with moisture. She had certainly never considered her son a sexual being or partner. In fact, her husband had a stroke three months ago, and the doctor told her not to have sex with her husband for six months going forward. She wasn't sexually frustrated. Her husband's fingers and her vibrator had provided all the sex she required.

The bouncing cock rubbing against her pussy slowly demanded her full attention. She couldn't help but squeeze her ass cheeks together to try to close her vagina opening, but it had the opposite effect.

It reminded her that a twenty-year-old cock was thrusting itself against the lips of her wet pussy.

Ellen felt what she thought was an answering thrust from Joel's penis to her movement.

"Why is that little brat coming on to me by flexing his cock against me," she wondered.

But instead of getting angry, she actually responded again by pushing against his rising rod. Minutes later, they whipped into the drive at the farm, and Ellen breathed a sigh of relief.

She had been dangerously close to starting something that could have ruined both their lives.

The road got a little rougher and the motion of the truck added a side-to-side sway to the jogging motion. Joel would have sworn the heat coming from her thighs and ass increased more and more. It couldn't have been more like fucking if they had been in a bed. Just when he was about to blow his load all over, they turned into the farm drive and the truck rolled to a stop.

"There," said Tasha, "that wasn't so bad a trip, was it?"

"I thought it was a perfect road trip," his mother said. She turned on his lap, grinding her ass against his hard cock, and slowly slid out of the truck to the ground, her dress sliding up until her panties were just peeking from underneath.

"I don't think Joel minded a bit. Did you honey?" *She turned to him and winked.*

He couldn't believe what she had said.

"Ah, no, I agree with you, it was just perfect. The time just flew by," he said.

"Great," Tasha said, "Why don't we go in and see where Dad wants this stuff put.

"Joel," his mom said, *"Why don't you stay out here and, ah, maybe untie the covering, you know, get things settled down.*" Her eyes flicked to his crotch and returned to his face.

He blushed when he realized his hard-on was standing out, tent-like, from the front of his shorts.

"Okay, I'll... I'll get things ready to carry in," he stammered.

She grinned and walked around the truck to join Tasha on her way to the house.

Within twenty minutes, the load was in the house, and they were ready to start going back home. But as usual when they visited grandma, she insisted they take some home-canned fruit home with them, so they ended up with three large cardboard boxes.

Just as they were loading them, it began to rain. Grandpa suggested we put the boxes in the truck to keep the cardboard from getting wet and falling apart, so once again there were boxes taking up the middle of the truck seat and Ellen had to ride on Joel's lap again. What a coincidence, as Tasha would have to drive.

They started

Within a short distance, Joel's cock achieved its original proportions and began rubbing her pussy. There was little doubt that he knew it was exciting for her.

If her panties hadn't slipped into her crack, and began rubbing her clit each time the truck bounced his cock against her, she would have been able to keep herself under control.

Actually, Ellen accidentally made the first thrust. Although later, she was to wonder if it had all been an accident. Her leg was falling asleep because of the odd angle she was holding it, and she raised her foot slightly to move it. The resulting loss of support for her ass allowed it to rest heavier on her son's cock.

When he pushed back in response, she was unable to keep her wet pussy from answering the hard rod tapping at its portal.

The trip home was slower due to the rain, but just as rough, and within the first mile, his hard-on was back in full force. His mom adjusted her ass so his rigid cock fit exactly between her legs and his cock was thrust tightly against her pussy. After a few rough jolts, he felt what appeared to be a soft push downward against his penis from his mom's ass.

It was hard to tell. He waited for a moment, then was sure he felt another push. For fear of being pushed, he was imagining things, doing a lot of wishful thinking. Then it happened again, and there was little doubt his mom was pushing her pussy against his hard-on. In answer, he flexed his cock.

He knew the movement would be so minor she would barely feel it, but if she had pushed, it would be enough, if she hadn't it wasn't so strong that it would feel like he was trying to fuck her if he had guessed wrong.

Immediately he felt an answering push. He answered with a strong thrust toward her pussy. Her response was immediate, and within seconds they were dry fucking. The boxes stacked between his aunt, him and his mother prevented her from seeing anything but their heads and shoulders. They were keeping the thrust below their waists. Joel first placed his hands on his mom's hips, then finally he reached around her and laid them on her thighs. Ellen inhaled sharply, but she continued to thrust her ass against his cock and flex her ass muscles, which was squeezing Joel's cock like a hand.

Joel began to slowly pull her skirt up her legs. He hoped to get his fingers under her panties for a quick feel. Just when Joel was about to blow his white cum in his shorts, they arrived back at their drive.

Ellen again twisted on his cock and slipped to the ground exposing her crotch-wet panties to him. He followed her out, and she reached for one of the boxes on the seat and handed it to Joel.

Here, honey, you can take this to the kitchen for me. Her smile told him she was again giving him a way to keep his hard-on out of sight.

"Thanks for all your help, you guys, I'll see you both get a reward for the effort," she said laughing.

"Hey, we enjoyed it. It was fun," Ellen said."

"I think Joel especially enjoyed the drive." Said Tasha.

Yeah, Aunt Tasha, I really enjoyed going out to the farm. It's fun to ride in a truck for a change instead of a car, it bounces around like a ride at Disney Land. "

"If they had rides like that at Disney Land," Ellen said, *"I'd have been there a long time ago."*

"Ah, you know what I mean, like a once in a lifetime thrill," he said.

"That I agree with," she said. Ellen was sure that it was in fact a once-in-a-lifetime thrill. It certainly couldn't go any further.

Joel carried the box inside and set it on the counter, then went into the room and grabbed the remote. He flicked the remote twice, and MTV started blasting from the screen. He chose a straight chair because he knew his mother would say something if he sat on the sofa in dirty shorts. Ellen followed him into the room. She stopped next to him.

"You didn't mind my sitting on your lap, did you?"

"No, mom. Like I told Aunt Tasha, the trip was a once-in-a-lifetime thrill."

"And my weight didn't bother you?"

"Mom, you don't weigh anything. I could hold you all afternoon and it wouldn't bother me. "

"Oh really? Maybe I'll take you up on that and sit on your lap now. "

Joel quickly looked up at her.

"I... I wouldn't mind that at all."

Ellen stared at him for a minute. My god, she thought, what am I doing? This is my son. If I sit on his lap, things are going to get out of hand. But her inner self convinced her that she was old enough to keep the situation from going past the point of mother and son joking around. Her eyes locked on his for a moment, then she stepped in front of him, and sat down on his lap. But this time her legs were outside Joel's and she was more open and exposed.

Joel couldn't believe that his mother had just spread herself and sat on his lap. It was an instant hard-on.

His cock rose quickly to lodge itself against her pussy, covered only by her thin dress and panties.

A moment later, she pushed down against his rigid boner, as she had been doing in the truck.

Joel thrust back. He makes little pretence of doing anything but pushing his cock against her pussy. She returned his thrust with one of her own. The thrusting continued, and there was no sham between them; they were dry fucking.

Joel reached his arms around Ellen (his mom) and laid his hands on her thighs. She looked down at them but said nothing. She was panting hard as she worked her ass against his hard member.

Joel began clutching bunches of her skirt in his fingers and, slowly, her skirt crept up her legs. Ellen watched her tanned legs become more exposed, but it felt like it was happening to someone else. Her mind was concentrating on the hard cock pressing against her inflamed pussy lips.

Finally, her panties came into view, and the dress continued up her body until Joel had bunched it at her waist. He lowered his hands back to her thighs and laid them with fingers pointing in on her legs just below her pussy.

Ellen stared but said nothing. Slowly his hands moved up, and she gasped as they touched her panty-clad mound.

Joel rubbed his mother's pussy and smeared the wet juice he found there around until her whole crotch was soaked in her flowing liquid. As her lips spread, he let his fingers move between them. He then traced an outline from the bottom of the puffy lips to her clit, which was clearly visible against her wet panties.

He flicked his finger against the nubbin, and Ellen groaned.

Joel lifted his hands and, pulling the waistband of her pants out with one hand, he slipped his other hand against her trembling belly and slid it down to her pussy.

Stopping there, he turned his palm upward and, with his other hand, thumbed her panties down over her hips.

Ellen's eyebrows were raised slightly as the panties slipped under her ass and crept to her knees. Joel didn't bother to remove them entirely. He liked to see the panties there to remind him that she was naked below the waist.

He pulled his hands back up her legs, and Ellen watched in awe as her son buried his fingers in between the puffy lips of her pussy, spreading them and slowly inserting two of his fingers into her channel.

Ellen's orgasm roared through her like a train through a tunnel, the sheer force scattering debris on both sides. She roared like an animal, huffed and puffed, and hunched her back on his fingers.

"Oh my god, I'm cuming on your fingers, mommy's cuming. Oh god, what have we done? "

Joel didn't wait for an answer. He lifted her up, forcing her to her feet while she was still out of control, and tore the buttons from his shorts, releasing his massive cock.

With much effort, he managed to pull the throbbing monster from his underwear, and suddenly there under Ellen was his eight-inch pillar of flesh, red-headed and throbbing.

The orgasm was so intense that Ellen didn't even know what Joel was doing. She was still foaming at the mouth and could barely stand in the position he had her in. Joel lowered her ass slowly. As she sat down, he positioned his cock directly below her dripping pussy. Ellen thought it was his fingers spreading the still burning lips of her hot cunt. But they kept spreading and spreading, and suddenly reality ate through her fogged brain.

She screamed. *Joel, No. No, you can't fuck me. "*

Joel released his support of her ass. With nothing holding her up and with her legs too weak to support her, she slipped down the massive shaft, taking the nine-inch cock into her saturated depths.

Oh, Ohh my god. Joel, *oh my God, you're so big.*

Ohh, you shouldn't be putting your cock in me. I'm your mother.

"Ellen's fall was stopped by Joel's legs. She was firmly impaled by the hard cock. "Unhh," she grunted."

Joel immediately lifted her a little and dropped her again on his shaft. burying it in her womb. Then again and again. It was a very hard fuck by Joel. He

96

fucked the hell out of his mom's wet pussy.

Moments later, Ellen was assisting him by raising and lowering herself on the red meaty pole. A couple of strokes later, Ellen's fingers strayed to her clit, and she began rubbing the stiffened little knob.

"God, Joel, you're a stud, a fucking horse."

Mom, I'm going to cum. I'm going to shoot. I'm going to shoot. "

Ellen threw her head back against Joel's shoulder.

"Me too, baby. Your cock is making me cum again. She said.

"Cum in my pussy, honey. Cum in mommy's cunt. "

"Ohhh, Mommmmm." Joel's cock spewed hot white threads of cumin into her.

Shoot your juice in, honey, shoot your juice in, mommy. Bury it in me. *"Uhhhhh."*

"Oh my god, you're fucking," Tasha screamed out.

"Joel, you're really fucking your mother?"

Ellen slumped back against Joel as her orgasm drifted off its peak.

She turned her head toward the voice coming from the kitchen door. "Not really, Sis," she said.

"You're wrong. We're really fucking each other, and if you think I'm going to let him take that massive cock out of me just because you've caught us, you're wrong. You can either watch and finger fuck yourself, or turn your head. " – **Ellen responded**.

Ellen turned as far around as Joel's cock would let her and planted a kiss full on her son's lips, her tongue slipping inside.

"Honey, your cock still feels hard. Why don't you fuck mommy again? We'll sort this all out later after we fuck. Unless you don't want to do it again."

For an answer, Joel lifted his mother's ass up about five inches, then dropped her.

Again, she was impaled on the massive rigid cock."

"Oh, honey. "Mommy loves the way you answer," she cooed.

…Continue to Series 4

What do you think would happen after Tasha caught Joel fucking his mom so hard, and what would Ellen do to keep this sacred secret from getting revealed by her sister?

Check out the continuation of this story in the fourth book in the series Our Secret 2 (Mother and Son's Secret Book 4).

Chapter 4

Our Secret is Exposed

A displeased Aunt Tasha was watching Joel from the kitchen door as he was getting his mother sexy and having her fucked so hard.

However, he was not pleased to know that his mother's sister was present to watch him drive a cock into his mother. He didn't know what she was going to do after the incident. He was concerned, deeply.

It was only then that he whispered,

"What if she tells someone?" to his mother.

The concern in Joel's voice told Ellen that his heart wasn't in the fucking anymore, but she was too busy bouncing up and down on his stiff rod to speak.

She grunted so that Tasha could hear her.

"She doesn't dare tell anyone," she said.

The fastest divorce you've ever seen will happen if

she does.

If she does, I have a tape that her husband will get.

Tasha pressed the issue, saying;

"You said you destroyed that tape. Didn't you?"

"I lied." Ellen said.

It's no secret that my husband has an interest in *voyeurism*. He likes to match the dog's style to your actions on the video-tape. True to his nature, I believe he would prefer to hump you if there were no repercussions for doing so.

She called her *"sick"* for claiming that her brother-in-law fucked her after he fucked his son. What extortion!

Joel inquired, *"What's on the tape?"*

"Your virtuous aunt is having sex with her husband's brother-in-law."

Tasha retorted,

"He wasn't my brother-in-law back then, and I was drunk."

If you fucked your husband's brother the night before your wedding, I don't think your husband would accept that as a justification.

On the night of a big party, my sister and her voyeur husband were parked in a nearby parking lot, taking pictures of the area.

Ellen, on the other hand, was preoccupied with her son's rod, her clit twitching, and the rising fluid in her belly, as she rode up and down the red flesh.

Joel's crotch was pressing against her uterus, and she had no idea what else to do with herself.

She'd never been so stuffed with a man's flesh before. Every woman's desire was to have a husband like hers, but she couldn't help but love her husband. She had the option to fuck him or not at any time.

Tasha; seeing her sister take part in such a taboo act only fueled the fire that was already raging within her.

Joel, please, please do it. Push it in. Give your entire cock to Mom. I'm going to cum again, baby.

I'm going to cum again. "

There was an exclamation of *"Ohhhhhhh Joeeel!"*

As she raised her feet and let all of her weight fall on Joel's lap, she drove his cock as far into her pussy as it was humanly possible to go, with a mournful cry.

Joel's enormous head was drenched in her fluid, which cascaded down his torso and onto his genitalia.

The fantastic orgasm that was coursing through her made her stop breathing for a brief moment before she snapped her head back against his shoulder and opened her mouth wide to take in the huge gulps of air that she desperately needed.

A hula dancer's ass kept on moving for the duration of her performance.

 She suddenly froze to the point of death. It was as if she had been subjected to a brutal beating. It was finally time for her dry, raspy voice to be heard.

"Oh Joel, that was the most amazing fuck I've ever had in my life. Anytime, not just now. "

Ellen leaned in and kissed him on the lips as she twisted on his lap.

Her tongue slid between his lips and became entwined with his own. He made her pussy twitch with his cock.

She leaned into his ear and said,

"I sensed that you haven't cum yet, have you, my son?"

Joel shrugged his shoulders.

Ellen leaned in and kissed him on the ear.

Tasha, why don't you fuck?

"No problem, and she'll never be able to tell anyone you fucked her." said Ellen to Joel.

"How, and would she accept it?" Joel asked.

"You can command her to do anything you want, but she will never disobey you because she has a fear of authority. It's just one of her oddities. Act as if you're in charge. If you try it, you'll see for yourself." – **Ellen** replied.

It took Ellen a while to get her feet back on the ground and slowly lift herself out of the enormous shaft.

The thought of fucking her son once more briefly crossed her mind, but she decided to wait until they had Tasha completely under their thumbs.

With her legs splayed wide in front of her son, Ellen slumped into the back cushions of the settee.

Joel's red-headed cock stood throbbing in the air as Ellen made her way toward the couch.

For the first time, Joel had a clear view of his mother's wet pussy. With each passing moment, the desire to bury his huge cock in that tight pussy becomes stronger.

Tasha was still in the doorway, staring at her nephew's enormous cock, and he gazed at her.

In Joel's stern voice, he ordered Tasha to join him.

Her expression was one of astonishment. *"What?"*

Joel repeated, *"I said, come over here."*

Tasha made her way across the room slowly and came to a halt next to him. His weaving wand, which he held in his crotch, caught her attention instead of his face.

A rapid increase in respiration caused Tasha's large breasts to expand.

This young woman had a slim figure with wide hips and nicely formed thighs. Her attire for the day was a short denim skirt and a white shirt.

Joel beckoned his aunt, "*Tasha*," to come closer. She didn't move until he said it a second time.

Tasha came within a few feet of him and sat down.

"*Pull up your skirt a notch,*" I said.

"*Joel!*" Tasha shrugged her shoulders.

"*Please, Aunt Tasha, don't make me ask you the same questions more than once. What did I tell you to do?* "

Her gaze never leaving his, she carefully raised the hem of her skirt till he could see her white pantyhose at the crotch.

"Pull up further," he ordered her.

Tasha rolled her eyes, but continued to raise the skirt.

Her entire pussy mound was now visible. A tell-tale damp spot could be seen where the material vanished between her legs.

A gentle touch from Joel's hand to stroke his cock made him more rigid and ready to bang his aunt.

He told her to *"pull off your pants now."*

Tasha said, *"Joel, nooooo,"* but her gaze was firmly fixed on his cocked grin. Lipped with saliva, she sat up straighter.

"Aunt Tasha, are you having any trouble hearing me?"
"Oh Joel," said Tasha.

Hooking her fingers into the waistband, Tasha pulled her underwear down to her calf and slid the panties down.

As she lowered her hands, her skirt fell.

Her pantie-falling legs dipped to her ankles, revealing her bare ankles. She pushed the panties aside with her toe as she stepped out of them.

"Okay, now you can raise your skirt," said Joel.

For the first time, Joel saw the swollen lips of Tasha's lightly hair-covered mound as she slowly emerged from the shadows.

In response, Joel pointed to the ceiling, and she raised her skirt higher, until she was exposed nearly to her waist.

Joel reached out and ran his finger along the moist slit, from bottom to top.

Tasha sighed and said, *"Oh, god."*

"Move closer to me." Joel ordered her.

When Tasha got close enough to his hip, he pushed her back away.

In order to get a better look at her, Joel removed the two buttons from her shirt and lifted it over her head.

Tasha's heart raced, but she remained silent. Her tits resembled two cones. She was wearing a thin bra, which showed off her hard nipples.

Joel instructed her to remove her bra.

Because he required her to follow his orders, it was not in his best interest to remove them himself.

She closed her eyes and unhooked the straps on her back. The bra slid down her arms to her wrists as she extended her arms forward. She threw it on the ground and opened her eyes wide enough to see him face-to-face.

Joel was in disbelief at the events that had transpired.

Now his stunning Aunt Tasha stood naked in front of him, as fresh as the day, after he had just fucked his mother.

Tasha tits were perfectly cone-shaped, something he'd only seen in magazines before.

He was close to shooting himself in the face in his rage. His crotch hardened.

The head was red-purple and swollen to a size he had never seen before, with ridges evident all the way down its length. He had a big hard-on, and Tasha gasped at the size of it.

"Tasha, sit on my lap like my mother did." Joel instructed her.

"She was doing it to you. But, I can't. She was sitting on your... your... your." Tasha said.

"Aunt Tasha, I was fucking her just like I'm going to fuck you."

"No, no no. You will not fuck me. I'm your aunt, and it's against the law to fuck a close relative. "

Inbreeding, on the other hand, isn't a good thing because it could lead to the development of undesirable traits. I recall you telling Mom that you couldn't get pregnant because you were on a new birth control pill.

"As a result, what's stopping us from getting a little fuck now? " Joel concluded.

Tasha uttered an agonized *"Ahhhhhhhhhhhhhhh."*

Then her gaze shifted to his quivering manhood, which was protruding from his crotch.

Again, she licked her lips to dryness. She felt a squirm in her pussy. She had no doubt that he was going to insert that huge cock into her at this point.

Her juices were gushing out of her pussy holes. She'd be dripping in a matter of seconds.

Her well-curved ass was cupped in Joel's right-hand side with his right hand. Her right leg was being drawn over his legs as he tightened her against him.

Tasha was surprised to find herself perched atop his monster dick.

With his right hand, Joel pressed down on the back of her head. As he lowered her right leg, he kissed her passionately on the lips.

When she opened her leg, she felt the head of his enormous cock gracing her pussy lips.

She pressed her lips to his and moaned. With his fingers on her ass again, Joel hauled her up into his lap and slouched down next to her. As he lowered her, her thighs clung to the outsides of his legs, causing her to slowly descend.

"Joel, my goodness. What are you doing to me, God? "

Tasha super-sized pussy lips was heavily stretched as Joel's huge and monster cock entered Tasha's flooded, wet pussy.

Ohhhh... Arrrrghhhhh… Huhhhh…… She screamed!

She trembled with fear.

During the orgasm, her scream rang out through the house. The first of many orgasms that she will remember for the rest of her life.

It was as though the weight of her head was squeezing through his aunt's narrow snout.

Even though she squeezed him so tightly, her hot oily fluid kept the passageway slippery, allowing him to glide until his cocked head was resting deep inside her juicy pussy.

She could not imagine it.

Joel fucked her mercilessly.

Joel increased the pace of the strokes he was giving to his aunt.

She moaned heavily as he was fucking her hard.

"Joel, oh Joel, oh Joel, pleasseeeee…… fuck me harder…."
-- Tasha was screaming.

"I'm on my way, I'm on my way!"

It took Joel some time to grasp that the second voice was coming from his mother, and he didn't know who it was at first.

Seeing his mother standing only a few feet away stroking her fingers in and out her wet pussy as she stared at his son cock in Tasha's hot cunt made him feel like an **Alpha male**.

I'm fucking your sister with the same wet cock that I fucked you with, Mom.

Honey, go ahead, *fuck her. Fuck her as hard as you can. She needs your huge cock.*

"When it comes to fucking her, the more fucking the better (so that our secret can remain within the three of us), but keep a little juice for me, honey." Ellen said.

Tasha whispered in Joel's ear,

"*Oh, Joel, stop talking and fuck me, fuck me like you will never do again in your lifetime*" as she wrapped her arms around his neck.

"*My feet are not on the ground, so you'll have to do all of the work.*" Tasha also said.

It's not a problem for us, Joel insisted.

His steps were measured, and Tasha's legs were wrapped around his hips as he slowly approached the center-of-the-room game table. He gently placed her back on the cloth-covered surface.

He said, "*Now you are in the perfect place.*"

Again, he slammed into her pussy with a full-force thrust, banging Tasha like he wanted her to pass-out.

With his aunt's pussy covered with fluid, he drew back and rammed his huge cock inside her, over and over again, much harder and faster.

Tasha arched her back in an effort to snag as much cock as she could get her hands on.

"Joel, fuck me, fuck me, fuck me. I am loving how you are fucking the hell out of my pussy." Tasha was asking for more!

Now I'm cuming, I am cuming Joel! "

Joel's heart was set off by her scream, and he felt the fluid in his tube finally begin to roll down.

Aunt Tasha, I feel the same way.... *I'm going to shoot your pussy with my cum.*

"Ohhhh. Ooh, that's good." Tasha responded.

When the enormous head spit forth juice, it bathed her pussy walls.

Joel felt like he was going to be pelted with bullets for the rest of his life.

Slushing out of her small hole, some of it ended up pouring down Tasha's backside, as he filled her to the brim with cum.

For Tasha, the thought of a man other than her husband, but her nephew's cum in her pussy was too much to bear, and as another orgasm jellied her insides, she burst into tears.

Joel backed across the room and sat down in his chair as soon as he removed his dripping shaft from her sweet pussy.

His mother (Ellen) sank to her knees and sucked his half-hard penis into her mouth as quickly as she could.

Tasha's legs were dangling lewdly off the table as she lay exhausted.

It's time to stop calling you *squirt*," Tasha remarked. I prefer the name *"Alpha - Gusher."*

It's like a cascade of your cum pouring out of me. It's a good thing I'm taking that heavy dose of your cum.

His mother's gaze was fixed on her son's penis, which was reviving itself.

Because I stopped taking the pill three months ago, we may now be referring to him as a father. It hadn't occurred to me that I'd be fucking anyone, not even my own son. But hey, *"it's too late now to be concerned about anything. "* **Ellen** said

"The only thing I ask is that you both call whenever you want to fuck." Jokingly, Joel responded.

They (Ellen & Tasha) chanted in unison, *"Count on it!"*

"What would you do if we were both pregnant? " Tasha inquired.

Joel gave a sly grin. A second and third set of sisters are waiting for you.

Can you imagine, *"Jeez, listen to him,"* she chuckled. *"Wow."*

She was eventually able to muster the energy to rise to her feet and turn to face Joel.

In response to his mother's head bobbing up and down, he threw his head back while thrusting his hips forward.

Is Joel really this serious? *"Damn,"* Tasha muttered.

"You really want to continue fucking," she said.

Joel could only nod in agreement.

If only we could fuck and suck together in the same bed.

"God, wouldn't that be a fun time?" Joel said.

It took her a moment to come to terms. Her response was to say,

"I'm all for trying to make it work, and maybe we could even attempt a bigger thing because I'm quite sure she swings both ways."

That was the spark that lit the fuse.

To make matters worse, Joel's crotch grew even

wider.

Joel screamed, *"Ohh mommmmm, I'm cumming, I'm cumming again."*

Ellen sank her face into his pubic hair and swallowed his cum, as her mouth and throat were flooded with the scent of his genitals.

The End!

Follow my Author profile and connect with me for more exciting ecstatic and romantic erotic stories.

Thank You!

Free Bonus

Grab My "At The Beach (Erotic Romance Story)" Ebook For FREE!

Today you can grab your copy of my Free Erotic Romance story e-book titled – **At The Beach**. Best of all, it won't cost you a thing.

Download and Subscribe for Free book, giveaways, and new releases by **Karena Donger.**

Click the image above to **Download the Book,** and

also Subscribe for Free books, giveaways, and new releases by me.

Or Follow the link below;

https://mayobook.com/karenadonger

As my subscriber, you will enjoy more free books exclusive to subscribers only, plus **Free Giveaways**. Wait no further, join my growing number of book lovers, and let's connect.

About The Author

I'm a romance writer and I've been writing for 10+ years. I write dark and romantic erotica. I have a penchant for romance. I also have a fondness for writing stories that inspire, and a love for the genre of romantic fiction. I write dark and erotic romance because I love the power of darkness and the eroticism that comes with it. I love the passion and the desire. I love the way a man will stop at nothing to get what he wants.

I also write fantasy and contemporary romance because I love the magic and adventure of it, coupled with the modern world and the characters in it. I love the modern family and modern relationships.

I have always loved reading romance novels, and now I am writing them too. I hope to share my love of romance with readers through my writing.

Visit https://mayobook.com/karenadonger to download my Free Erotic story **"At The Beach"** Today!

Other Books

1. The Road Trip (Mother and Son's Secret Book 1)

2. The Road Trip 2 (Mother and Son's Secret Book 2)

3. Our Secret (Mother and Son's Secret Book 3)

4. Our Secret 2 (Mother and Son's Secret Book 4)

5. The Road Trip Secret, Complete Series Box Set (Mother and Son's Secret)